Karen

Love,
Rhoda
April, 1973

THE
BLUE
CABOOSE

By

Dorothy Hamilton

Illustrated by Jerry Needler

HERALD PRESS, SCOTTDALE, PENNSYLVANIA
1973

Library of Congress Cataloging in Publication Data

Hamilton, Dorothy, 1906-
  The blue caboose.

  SUMMARY: After his father leaves to look for
steady employment, Jody and his mother worry about
supporting themselves and finding a cheaper place to
live.
  [1. Family life — Fiction]   I. Needler, Jerry,
illus. II. Title.
PZ7.H1836Bl   [Fic]   72-5474
ISBN 0-8361-1695-X
ISBN 0-8361-1696-8 (pbk.)

THE BLUE CABOOSE

Copyright © 1973 by Herald Press, Scottdale, Pa. 15683
Library of Congress Catalog Card Number: 72-5474
International Standard Book Number: 0-8361-1695-X
Printed in the United States
Designed by Alice B. Shetler

To the Boys and Girls
Whom I Have Tutored

JODY

Jody Bryant reached for a pillow to put over his head. He'd done this about every morning since his father came home from Vietnam. Sometimes he did it at night for the same reason. To shut out the noise of the radio or the yelling.

This time was different. Jody opened his eyes and propped himself up on one elbow. It was morning all right. Shafts of spring sunshine came in the high window above his bed. But there wasn't any noise -- or not much anyway. Just a swish of running water, then a couple of clanks of a pan.

Jody sat up.
It's so quiet!" he thought.

"Maybe Dad's finally been able to forget about the war and get some sleep," Jody thought. "I sure hope so!"

Then he heard his mother calling from the kitchen. "Jody! Time to get up." Usually she came to his bed and shook him gently. Or she shut the door to the living room where his dad lay around a lot even though he didn't sleep much.

After he'd dressed in clean Levis and T-shirt, Jody walked on tiptoe into the next room. It looked different. There were no rumpled blankets or doubled-up pillows on the bed. It was folded up to look like a couch.

His mother was putting steaming oatmeal into a blue bowl.

"You'd better hurry," Lillian Bryant said. "I overslept. It was so quiet."

"I noticed," Jody said. "Where's Dad?"

He kept his eyes on his mother as he pulled out the chair. "If she's worried I can tell by her eyes," he thought.

Jody's mother had sounded pretty cheerful since his dad came home, even after he'd lost his fourth job. But lately the clouded look in her eyes hadn't gone away.

"Well, I guess I might as well tell you," Mrs. Bryant said. "Your father's left for somewhere."

"You mean to look for another job?" Jody asked. He carefully sifted a spoonful of brown sugar over the hot oatmeal and watched it melt to a caramel color.

"Maybe," his mother said. "But not around here. He left a note. It seems someone told him veterans get a better break farther west."

Jody didn't say anything for awhile, but he wished he could say what he was thinking. What would be so wrong about his mother telling him if she was worried? He knew anyway. Or didn't she realize that? Was he still just a little kid to her?

She sat down across the table from him. He looked straight into her eyes. They weren't cloudy, at least not now. "It's no secret that your father's been

10

real restless since he came back. He's a changed man. Maybe we would be too if we'd have gone through what he did." She stirred her tea and added, "He left us what money he had and I figured I can get some work to do."

Jody glanced at the clock and hurried to finish his milk.

"We might look for a smaller place to live," his mother said. "We could make out with two rooms. Farther out of town rent might be cheaper."

The place where they were didn't seem very big to Jody. The living room had once been the square kitchen of the big old house on South Walnut Street. His bedroom used to be the pantry, and the old back porch was now the place where his mother cooked.

Jody remembered when the Bryants moved into the apartment. He had asked, "What's a pantry?" when the owner told them how the three rooms had been used. He'd been puzzled by the explanation that a room was needed to store food. Who ever had that much?

Jody's mother sipped her tea and kept on talking. It was nice to hear her. She didn't need to whisper or talk low for fear his dad would be upset by what she said or that he'd say she was keeping secrets or something.

"I've been sort of looking around for work," she said. "But -- well, Barney got all upset if I so much as mentioned the word "job." A man's pride has thin skin, I guess. Anyway, we got enough money to keep us going while I look into the matter."

A ray of sunlight slid into the kitchen. It made glints of light on the glass salt-shaker.

"You going out looking for the job today?" Jody asked. "Or a place to live?"

"The job," his mother said. "Our rent's paid up here until a week from Saturday. Now you scoot off to school. I'll be here when you get home."

"OK," Jody said. He felt good. Relieved. Maybe it wasn't right for a guy to feel

12

good because his dad was gone. He hadn't been before –– when the reserve unit was called up and sent to Vietnam. But now it was different –– his dad wasn't the same.

Jody didn't think much about what might be going to happen after he got to school. The sun seemed to make everything a little better and more fun. It had been rainy and chilly for over a week.

The fifth-grade section of the playground seemed to bounce at recess and at noon. Boys jumped in the air catching and throwing balls of all sizes. Others ran and hurdled the railings which fenced in James Whitcomb Riley School.

Even some of the girls were livelier. They didn't act so grown up. One group circled on the swaying clanking maypoles and four jumped rope.

His father's leaving and the thought of moving faded out of Jody's mind until he started home. His friend Carlos, who was in the other fifth grade, was waiting at the end of the walk. One boy almost always waited on the other.

"What you doing tonight?" Carlos asked.

"Nothing special, I guess," Jody said. "Why? You got something in mind to do?"

"Well, it's warm and we've not been over to the bridge for a long time," Carlos said.

"I know," Jody answered. "I wonder if the high water washed away our cave in the bank." The boys had played in the grassy hollow for two summers since Carlos had gone to Riley School. The shady cave was cool even in August when the Indiana air was heavy with the heat.

"I'll have to ask my mom if I can go," Jody said.

"Me too," Carlos said. "Wait up!" They were at the end of the street where the Mendez family lived in a big attic which had been made into an apartment. It was really one big room with a tiny kitchen in one dormer window and a bathroom in the other. Curtains separated rooms.

Carlos ran up the wooden stairs on the side of the house and came back down

14

after three to four minutes. "I can go," he said. "But I have to come home when the freight train whistles. My mamma works nights at the diner this week. And Papa has to stay at the filling station a while."

"That means you have to watch your little brother," Jody said.

"Not by myself," Carlos answered. "My mamma would not leave us alone. We go to my grandmother's."

When the boys crossed the alley behind Jody's home, Carlos said, "I'll wait here while you ask."

Jody knew why. His dad hadn't been friendly toward Carlos the one time he'd gone inside. And he'd done a lot of yelling afterward about Mexicans coming up here and taking jobs.

Jody had tried to say that Mr. Mendez was an American and that he'd always lived in Texas. But his dad hadn't listened.

"Come on in," Jody said. "No one's here but my mother and me now."

"Oh," Carlos said. He didn't ask any questions. But he did follow Jody into the small kitchen.

Mrs. Bryant was ironing in the living room. Men's shirts hung on chair backs and on the wall.

"Whose are they?" Jody asked. These were all white and his father didn't wear anything but old army shirts.

"I really don't know," his mother said. "Mrs. Prescott takes on ironings and has more than she could do. So this is my first job."

Jody asked if he could go across the empty lots to the bridge over White River.

His mother's eyebrows went up. "I don't know if I should say yes or not. The water's probably pretty high. Because of all the rain."

"But we won't do crazy stuff," Jody said. "Like hang over the railing or walk on the boards that stick out over the river."

"Well! I should hope not!" his mother said. "You may go. But when you hear the 5:15 whistle blow come back to the old factory and meet me."

"What will you be doing over there?" Jody asked.

"I thought since it's nice out," she said, "we'd walk over toward South Gharkey and look for a place to live."

"OK," Jody said. "We have to come back when the freight train goes through anyway. Carlos has to go home then."

"Grab some jelly doughnuts as you go out," his mother said. "I got them at the second-day store. But they're pretty fresh."

"Thanks!" Jody said.

"Gracias!" Carlos echoed.

2

The boys crossed Walnut Street when red lights stopped evening traffic between Twelfth and Sixteenth streets. They walked by way of the vacant lots and went around the old factory. The grass was beginning to show green through the tangled dry mat. Weed stalks brushed against their legs.

"This'd be a nice park if it was cleaned up," Carlos said.

"Yeah," Jody said. "It's the only place not crowded with houses and stores and stuff."

"And there are trees over there by that old railroad car. I wonder why no

18

one builds over here?" Carlos asked.

"My mom says it's because Mr. Gable won't sell. He owns it. You know him. He runs the store."

"I know," Carlos said. "And the laundromat. He probably could get a bunch of money for all this land."

"Maybe he doesn't need more money," Jody said.

"I guess some people don't," Carlos said.

They came to Liberty Street and went south to the bridge. There wasn't much traffic over here. The street was rutted and bumpy. People liked to drive where it was smoother.

The boys leaned on the rusty railing and watched the sand-colored water as it rushed and tumbled downstream. They couldn't see the bottom of the river and the only rocks in sight were sticking out of the bank.

"It sure is muddy," Jody said.

"Si," Carlos answered. "It's not a white river now," Carlos said. "Why would

"It sure is muddy," Jody said.
"Si," Carlos replied.
"It's not a white river now!"

anyone give it such a name?"

"Long ago the water was probably clear," Jody said. "And once in a while it is now. But not much."

"I can't tell if our cave's still down there. Can you?" Carlos asked.

"No. The water's too high and the brushes hide the place," Jody said.

The boys didn't stay long. Watching the water wasn't as much fun when they couldn't see the riverbed and the smooth stones.

They headed back toward Walnut Street several minutes before the freight train whistled at the crossing to the west. A puff-tailed rabbit crossed their path in springy jumps.

Then Carlos tripped and nearly fell. "My toe caught on something hard."

Jody kicked at clumps of dead grass and bent over. "There's an old railroad track down here."

"Where does it go, I wonder?" Carlos asked.

"Up to the factory maybe. Up to the ca-

22

boose. Let's follow it."

"But I don't understand," Carlos said. "How did the caboose get over there? The track starts here."

"Now it does. But it used to join up with the main line. Mr. Gable told me. He called this a siding. I asked him once."

The boys tried to walk on the rusty rails. But weeds and grass kept getting in their way. Jody looked around once to see if his mother was walking up the cinder drive.

The boys came to the caboose.

"Let's look inside," Carlos said. "I always wanted to see how it looked."

"OK," Jody said. "I already have. You can go on in. I do sometimes."

"Why?" Carlos asked. "Is it a hideout or something?"

"No," Jody said. "And no one's supposed to bother around. But I always ask Mr. Gable before I come over here to play."

"All by yourself?" Carlos asked.

"Yes," Jody said. "I used to like to pretend it was on the end of a real

"Hey, Jody, that old caboose could be
our hideout!"

train. That I was really going places. Of course that was when I was a little kid."

"I'd like that," Carlos said. "Even now. Do you reckon Mr. Gable would let me?"

"Sure. If you ask," Jody answered.

"Do you suppose he'd care if I just looked now?" Carlos asked.

"No. I'll go with you."

They walked to the end of the car and climbed up on the platform. Carlos said trainmen must have long legs to step up so high. The door inched open with a squeaky sound. Cobwebs hung in the corner and the boys' feet stirred up puffs of dust. Some of it rode on beams of light after Jody rubbed a spot on one of the west windows.

"There's more room here than I thought," Carlos said.

"I know," Jody answered. "It's almost as big as two of the rooms where we live. Bigger than two others."

As they left the caboose Jody saw his mother standing at the end of the deserted factory.

"I'd better go," Carlos said. "Your mamma's coming and that evening train will be passing any minute. See you manana."

Jody and his mother walked up and down Gharkey Street. They saw only two For Rent signs. One apartment was two rooms upstairs. Mrs. Bryant shook her head as they climbed the narrow steps. "I don't think this is what we want. Nothing is clean. Not the halls or yard or the alley. I couldn't do all the cleaning for everyone."

The second place was a little better, but too large. They needed one less room, instead of four.

"Will we stay where we are?" Jody asked as they headed toward Walnut Street.

"Oh, I've not given up yet," his mother said. "There are other streets."

"You know something," Jody said as they walked into the shadowed apartment. "I'm hungry. It seems like half a day since I ate that jelly doughnut."

26

"Probably so," his mother said. "I tell you what, I'll give us a little treat with some of the ironing money. You run over to the store and get a pint of ice cream while I scramble eggs and make toast."

Jody didn't see anyone on his way to the store. No one was bouncing a basketball in backyards or knocking out flies in the alley. He knew some families with dads went uptown a lot and the tenth of the month was payday for some people.

Mr. Gable was stacking cans of pork and beans on a shelf.

"What can I do for you, Mr. Jody Bryant?" the tall man asked.

"I'd like a pint of ice cream," Jody said. "Dutch chocolate please."

Mr. Gable slid the frosty carton into a brown sack and counted out change for the dollar.

Jody started toward the door, then suddenly he stopped, turned, and asked, "Does the old caboose belong to you, Mr. Gable?"

"Not exactly," Mr. Gable said. "But I reckon it'll stay on my property till it falls apart. Why?"

Jody shrugged his shoulders. "I don't know why I asked. Just wondered, I guess. Well, I'd better go before this ice cream melts. See you."

He liked the quiet of the evening. Usually the neighborhood was noisy. There was a lot of traffic and it seemed like no one had a car that didn't rattle or roar or backfire. And buses came around from Madison to Walnut. Their choking smoke and rumbling wasn't exactly pleasant. But for a little while almost everyone was away or inside.

Jody became sleepy soon after he'd finished eating. He had a hard time holding his eyelids up until he finished doing his homework. Fractions were easy for him to understand when he wasn't too drowsy to think.

He curled up on the couch while his mother dampened the second basket of ironing sent to her by Mrs. Prescott. He could hear little thumps as she rolled shirts and dresses into tight bundles. But he didn't hear many bumps before he sank into sleep.

Suddenly he became aware that a man

was talking to his mother at the back door. "Has Dad come back already?" Jody wondered. "No, that's Mr. Gable."

Jody sat up and rubbed his eyes. His mother came in and said, "Well, Sleepyhead! Did you wake up in time to go to bed?"

"What did Mr. Gable want?"

"Oh! You heard him? Well, another job came to me. Without my even hunting it." She went on to say that Mrs. Gable couldn't get around very well yet because of her fall on ice. "And she wants me to clean and cook two hours a day."

"But what if you find an all-day job?" Jody asked.

"I brought that up," his mother said. "But Mr. Gable said not to be in too big a hurry about hunting one. Said he had something else in mind. That it would take a little time to work it out."

"I wonder what."

"I don't know," his mother said. "But I'm grateful for as much as two hours. Now you scoot off to bed."

"I'm not so sleepy now," Jody said.

"Well you'll be in the morning. And it's already half past nine."

Jody lay awake for a while. He could see the moon out the high window. It looked like half a circle of pale gold tissue paper. But astronauts couldn't walk on thin paper.

After a while pictures began to move around in his mind. They were a little like dreams. Only his eyes were still open. And he could see the caboose plainly, as if he was standing inside it.

It was like he was living in the railroad car. There were chairs and beds and a table. And his mother was there. She was moving around doing something.

Then Jody suddenly sat up in bed. "I'm not dreaming," he thought. "I'm thinking." He jumped out of bed and went to the living room. His mother was spreading a blanket on the opened-out couch.

"Jody! What are you doing out of bed? Is something wrong?"

"No," Jody said. "But I had to get up.

I just had an idea."

"What in the world are you talking about?" his mother asked.

Out in the bright light Jody's excitement began to fade. "Maybe Mom'll laugh at me," he thought. "Grown-ups don't always see things the same as kids. But I might as well say it -- now that I've started."

"I was about asleep," he said. "I guess I was thinking about those apartments we saw. And what we could do -- you know what I mean -- about a place to live."

"Yes," his mother said, "I was thinking about the same thing. But go on --"

"Well, Carlos and I went in the old caboose this evening and things sort of went together. Why couldn't we live in the caboose -- in the summer anyway?"

His mother looked surprised but she didn't laugh. She ran one little finger back and forth on an eyebrow. She did this a lot when she was figuring stuff out -- like problems.

"Would you like that?" she said after what seemed like a long time. "I mean if we could. We don't even know who owns the caboose."

"I do. Mr. Gable does, in a way," Jody said. "I asked him."

"I never really saw the inside of such a car," his mother said. "I wouldn't have any idea of how roomy they are."

"There's more'n you think," Jody said. "As big as the kitchen and my room and some to spare. And people live in smaller spaces –– like the small house trailers over in Echo Park."

"Well, I suppose that's true," his mother said.

They talked for nearly half an hour.

Mrs. Bryant said the rent would probably be a lot less and that maybe they'd be able to save money.

"Besides, Mom, I think it would be fun," Jody said. "There are trees over there and grass. Do you suppose we could?"

"Well, we can see about it," his mother said. "It won't cost anything to ask."

Jody wanted to ask if he'd made his mother feel good. She was always thinking of ways to help him and to protect him. Would it upset her to know he was trying to do the same for her? Or was it more important for her to think she was doing a good job of taking care of him -- being a parent for two people?

He didn't say any of these things, but he did ask, "Then you don't think my idea's bad or clunky?"

"No, Jody," his mother said as she got up and ran her hand back and forth across his shoulders. "In fact, it might be about the best idea anyone around here's had for a long time. We'll see. Good night, Jody-boy."

"Good night, Mom."

This time Jody went to sleep almost as soon as he pulled the soft blanket up around his shoulders.

The next thing he knew it was morning and his mother was calling him to breakfast. He glanced at the clock as he sat down to eat. "It's late," he said.

"I know," his mother answered. "You were sleeping so soundly that I hated to call you until the last minute."

She went on to ask Jody to wash his breakfast dishes. She was going on over to work for Mrs. Gable.

"I thought maybe you'd ask about the caboose first," Jody said.

"I thought of it," his mother said. "But Mr. Gable's always so busy this time of morning. Selling tablets and pencils and penny candy."

"You can't buy much for a penny now, Mom."

"Well. Whatever."

"I sure would like to know what Mr. Gable will say," Jody said.

"You will," his mother said. "I'll have some idea by noon. I'll run over to the store as soon as I've finished the house-work. Want me to come to the school playground?"

Jody thought for a minute but not any longer. "Yes. I wish you would. I can't wait until evening." Maybe the other kids would make fun and call him a mamma's baby. Kids like Tony. Right now Jody didn't care what anyone said. Except Mr. Gable. "And I sure hope he says yes."

The gold hands on the schoolroom clock seemed to crawl around the white circle that morning. Jody had to force himself to keep working and paying attention. And he even hurried eating lunch, which was one of his favorite school meals. Hot dogs, macaroni with cheese, and fresh fruit salad. "I can't wait on Carlos today. I have to see if Mom's out there -- and hear what she has to say."

At first Jody thought his mother had forgotten about her promise. Or that maybe she didn't have anything good to tell him. He was nearly to the white stakes on either side of the end of the walk before he saw her hurrying toward him. "I should've known she'd come," he thought. "She always keeps promises."

Jody could tell that the news was good as soon as his mother came close enough so that he could see her face. She looked happy and excited.

She shook her head as she came across the street. "Things have really happened fast," she said. "It's all settled. We can move in when we get the caboose cleaned up."

"Great!" Jody said. "Will it cost very much?"

"No. That's the best part," his mother said. "Mr. Gable said he wouldn't feel right charging anything. And that if we were brave enough to try and make our own way he'd be willing to give us a boost, as well as some paint."

"Paint?"

"Yes. He got a bargain when he painted the store and laundromat last summer. But he bought too much and has a lot left over. It's blue."

"A blue caboose," Jody said. "I guess they are blue sometimes."

"Anyway, this one will be," his mother said. "Well, I'd better run along. I've got things to see to and you'd better get back to school."

"When will we move?" Jody asked.

"As soon as we make the place fit to live in," his mother said. "And the longer

I stand here, the longer that'll take. Come straight home."

"I will," Jody answered. "See you."

He went around the building to look for Carlos. He had to tell someone what was going to happen. But something told him not to blab the news to everyone that he was going to live in a caboose. Kids could say some mean things about good stuff. Some kids did anyway. And grown-ups too, sometimes.

Carlos was leaning against the back of the building watching some boys play softball. He smiled when he saw Jody. "Hi, amigo," he said. "I thought maybe you'd decided to skip school."

"No," Jody said. "But I'd sure like to for once." Then he told Carlos the whole story. He didn't even leave out the part about his dad leaving them. "So Mom and I are on our own."

"Don't you have family around here?"

"No," Jody said. "My dad's folks came from Tennessee to work in a factory. They went back and Dad stayed.

And Mom's family's all dead, I guess. All but an aunt in Colorado or someplace."

"Well, anyway, I think living in a caboose would be bueno," Carlos said. "And there's grass and trees over there. And not so much noise as here."

"I know," Jody said. "Why don't you see if you can go over with me tonight? We might even work on it."

"I will ask," Carlos said as someone began ringing the end-of-noon-hour bell.

As soon as Jody reached the apartment that evening, his mother sent him back to the store for empty cardboard boxes.

"I thought maybe we'd begin cleaning up the caboose," he said.

"We will start early tomorrow morning," his mother said. "It's Saturday. Remember? We should get a lot done in a whole day. Get it ready to move in, maybe."

"Even paint?"

"No. Not that much," his mother said. "We can paint after we're over there. The quicker we move, the more we save on living expenses. Now you scoot. I want to pack what we won't use for a few days."

When Carlos came, Mrs. Bryant gave the boys a cloth measuring tape, a stub of a pencil, and a small pad of paper. "Measure the caboose and write down the figures," she said. "So I'll know how much furniture we can take. And how much we can try to sell."

"Sell?"

"Yes. I talked to Mr. Gable. The secondhand man is his brother-in-law. He's getting in touch with him. We'll go to the grocery before it closes and see when he can come look at what we don't need."

When the boys came back and Carlos went home Jody's mother studied the measurements and did some figuring while Jody ate a sandwich and tomato soup.

"We can make beds and couches out of your bunk beds," she said, "and sell the sofa -- and that chest of drawers and a few chairs -- and the stove."

"The stove?" Jody said. "Won't we cook over there?"

"Not with gas," his mother said. "No pipeline runs across the lots. So I'll buy a small oil stove. Secondhand, I hope."

As they left to go to see Mr. Gable, Jody's mother said. "I don't know how much we'll get for what we can't use. But every little bit helps."

"Are we about out of money?"

"Oh, no," his mother said. "I still have the thirty-seven dollars your dad left plus a little more. My ironing and cleaning money has more than fed us and paid the light bill besides."

Mr. Gable was waiting on a customer when they walked in the door. This wasn't a serve-yourself market. Here the store-keeper wore a white apron and weighed sugar, sliced meat, and tied up packages with white string which unrolled from a cone.

Jody and his mother walked to the back and sat on one of the long seats that joined at a corner. "These are like the church pews in Cedar Branch," Mrs. Bryant said. As she ran her palm up and down a curved arm.

"Cedar Branch? Where's that?" Jody asked. "You never talked about this place before."

"Didn't I? Well, maybe I should have. It's where I went to church all my growing-up days. Before I married and came to Fort Jefferson to live."

"I remember going to church once," Jody said. "When Dad was fishing or something."

"Only once? Is that all you remember?" his mother asked. "But I guess you were too little to recall when I went regular -- before -- "

Jody saw that his mother's eyes were wet and glistening. She was about to cry. Why?

"Before what?" he asked. He didn't want her to cry. But he had to know what she was remembering. Was it a good or bad thing which brought tears to her eyes?

His mother smiled and shook her head. "Before I let your dad talk me into staying at home. But I never did agree that going was a waste of time. I just quit fighting him on the subject. But I missed going for a long time -- the singing and the good feeling. But then I got in the habit of staying away."

Mr. Gable turned the Closed sign around so it faced the street. Then he came back and sat down on the other seat. "Well, it's all set," he said. "My brother-in-law's going over to look at your things when he closes tomorrow night."

"That's fine," Jody's mother said. "I really appreciate all you're doing."

"No need for thanks," Mr. Gable said. "Now don't forget. You'll run into problems. There's no electricity over there for one thing."

Mrs. Bryant said she'd planned to buy a kerosene lamp and an oil stove. And Mr. Gable told them he was having water turned on in an outside faucet at the end of the old factory.

The tall man shook his head. "It hurts me to remember the days when the plant was running. And to see the buildings run down."

"Why did you close it? I've often wondered," Mrs. Bryant asked.

"Oh, it's the times. People restless. Never satisfied," Mr. Gable said. "I couldn't meet the wage demands. I reckon I wasn't a good enough manager. Maybe I was cut out to be a groceryman, not a gear manufacturer."

Jody's mother bought a box of soap powder and some bananas and cookies for the next day. Mr. Gable loaned them a heavy broom and two scrub brushes for cleaning the caboose.

Jody packed his model planes and his four Andy Hardy books and his games while his mother finished an ironing. He wouldn't have any time to play or read for a few days.

As he started to his room to go to bed he said, "It's going to be something like going camping."

"You like that idea?"

"Sure! I've heard kids talk about it

and tried to picture how it'd be."

He drifted off to sleep thinking about the grass and the trees.

5

The next thing Jody knew his mother was rubbing her hand back and forth across his forehead. He opened his eyes, blinked, and shut them again. Sunbeams slanted in the narrow window.

"Is it late?" he asked. "That sun's so bright."

"I took the drapes down," his mother said. "But jump up! It's time we got this day moving."

Jody leaned over and pulled his sneakers from under the bed.

"Your clean Levis are on the ironing board," Mrs. Bryant said. "I'm going on over. You bring the bucket and brushes when you come. And eat your cereal and drink your milk!"

Jody dressed in a hurry. As he went to the kitchen he caught a glimpse of his mother going around the house. She was carrying a broom, a mop, and a basket. "Our lunch maybe," he thought.

He was locking the back door when someone yelled, "Hey, Bryant! Come on over. Play ball."

Jody turned to see Tim LeMasters and Tony Morelli going down the alley. Tim had been a good friend. At least that's how Jody had felt for a long time. Then Tony moved into the house next door and Tim began to hang around with him. Now things seemed different.

"I can't," Jody said. "We might move and I've got to help my mom."

"Where you movin' to?" Tony asked.

Jody started to say, "In the old caboose." But for some reason he stopped. He didn't understand why. He'd told Carlos the exciting news. And he'd have probably told Tim and not felt one bit uneasy. But with Tony around it was different. Why? Maybe because he was always putting everyone down.

Tony had a kind of twisted look on his face when any of the guys mentioned any of the others. And he had a sharp way of saying, "They're not such a much!"

Jody didn't want to see Tony's face or hear his voice when he heard that the Bryants were living in a caboose. He'd say a lot. No one could stop him. "But if I don't see or hear him things won't be spoiled," Jody thought.

So he just said, "Over toward Liberty Street."

Jody thought of going down to see Carlos. But he knew that Mrs. Mendez worked until early morning and would be asleep. It wouldn't be right to waken her. Then he saw his friend's grandmother leaving the grocery.

Jody put the bucket of brushes on the narrow step and ran to the end of the alley. "Mrs. Santos," he called. "Will you give Carlos a message if you see him?"

"Si," the dark-eyed lady said. "When he opens his eyes to see me, what shall I say?"

"Tell him to come over to the old caboose when he has time," Jody said. "I will be there about all day, I think. He knows why."

As he came within sight of the car he saw puffs of dust coming out the door and the two windows which were broken. His mother was already busy.

Much work was done before the sun was overhead. The boards of the old bunks were broken and loose. It was easy to rip them away from the sides of the car and carry them outside to be burned. His mother piled the last of the wooden slats on his outstretched arms.

"I think your bunk bed will fit fine," Mrs. Bryant said.

"Mom! Whoever sleeps on top could rub his nose on the ceiling. And probably wouldn't be able to turn over."

His mother smiled. "Take that load outside and I'll explain what I have in mind."

As Jody swept up the splinters and bent nails he heard the plan. "It's a good thing the sections of your bed come apart and that they're youth size. And that I'm not very tall. We can put one along this side. And the other across the end. Making an around-the-corner couch."

She went on to say that the drapes could be hung across the end to hide their clothes and make a dressing room. "We may have to climb over a bed to get to this clothes closet. But that will keep us spry and limber."

By noon the caboose was swept, dusted, and scrubbed. Even the small cupboards where the railroad crews had kept supplies, pans, and dishes were clean. Newspapers were folded to line the shelves.

"It looks bigger -- now that it's clean," Jody said.

"There is more room than I figured," his mother said. "I think we can bring my rocker and your little desk. It wouldn't be home without them. And the table with the folding leaves and two or maybe even three chairs. So we can have company."

They'd washed the layer of dust from their hands and faces when Carlos walked up on the back platform which Jody called the mini-porch.

"Hi," Carlos said. "What's going on?"

Mrs. Bryant smiled and said, "Come in if you want, Carlos. And look around."

"Yeah," Jody said. "I wanted you to come over."

Carlos walked through the car and looked out the windows. His brown eyes sparkled as he turned and said, "This is neat! Like a giant camper."

"Yes. I guess it is," Jody's mother said. "Maybe not as fine, and it won't be going anywhere. But it's roomy and solid. Now why don't we go out in the sun and eat our lunch and you and Jody can talk the whole thing over?"

Carlos said he wasn't hungry but before long he was eating a peanut-butter sandwich.

The sun was warm and the grass under the umbrella-shaped trees was thick and green. They could see cars over on Walnut Street. But they were far enough away from the heavy Saturday traffic so that its noise was muffled.

"It's nice over here," Carlos said. "Almost like country."

"I know," Mrs. Bryant said. "I like that. Mr. Gable's going to loan us a lawn-mower to mow a patch for a yard. And these two trees will give us shade."

"And we're going to paint the caboose," Jody said. "Blue."

"That's a poem," Carlos said. "The blue caboose."

The boys began making rhymes. Carlos put music to the words and sang about a boy who lived in a blue caboose who tripped on a noose, bought a goose, and rode a moose.

Mom said, "We're not going to paint before we move. I can do that almost as easy afterward. And moving in a hurry will save us money. We'll get a few days rent back. If the weather stays nice, we can move soon."

"Great," Jody said. "I'm ready."

"Well, maybe so," his mother answered. "But the caboose isn't. And we have things to do in the apartment. So let's get busy."

Carlos stayed with them until there was no more to be done on the car. The walls were washed with soapy water so that the paint wouldn't be streaked by dust. A man came to put in new window glass and all four panes were polished until they sparkled in the spring sunshine.

6

Saturday evening was a busy time for
Jody and his mother. They started to
pack, then Mrs. Bryant said, "I don't
think we're putting first things first. As
my granddad would have said, 'We've got
the cart in front of the horse!' "

It was her idea that they should go see
the man at the secondhand store about a
stove and talk to him about what they had
to sell. "Then it'll be easier to separate
the takings from the leavings," she said.

They changed into clean clothes and
left two loads in the washers at the
laundromat. As Jody's mother put it,

"There's no good in lugging dirt across the lot, then back again."

They hurried around the corner and up to the corner of Hayt and Twelfth. The store door was open but it was shadowy inside. Piles of used tables, chairs, and cupboards blocked out the light of evening.

Jody walked down the narrow aisle toward the back. He could see a dim light, coming from a single bulb dangling from the ceiling. Then he heard voices and bumping sounds.

"Lift up on that end," someone yelled. "It's hung up on the doorsill."

Jody went around a stack of tall bookcases and saw a wide-open door. Two men were pulling on a piano and one was yelling at whoever was on the other end. "Lift. Then shove."

Suddenly the heavy piece of furniture came up and forward. And a short square-shouldered man caught a glimpse of Jody and his mother.

"Howdy, folks," he said. "Looking for something?"

56

"For you," Mrs. Bryant said. "If you're Mr. Mandelle."

"I am. You buying or selling?"

"Both," Jody's mother said. Jody walked around as she explained that she was looking for a smaller stove and had a couch and a few other things to sell. A lot of stuff there looked like junk to Jody. There were many things besides furniture. He saw two sleds with rusty runners and a doll buggy with one bent wheel. There was even a bike. No, there were parts of more than one.

As he wandered back toward his mother, Mr. Mandelle said, "I think I got something you can use in the way of a stove. Come out here in the shed."

Jody wondered how the owner knew where things were, or even what he had.

"This is a combination heater and cooker -- using oil," the man said. "This side has a coil burner down low for a space heater. And there's the cooking burners and the storage space below on this side.

'Course there's only two burners and no oven," he said.

"Well, I can make out," Jody's mother said. "Are you sure it works?"

"It will before we make a deal," Mr. Mandelle said. "I'll try to get over and look at your stove and other stuff in about an hour. Soon as my wife comes in to wait on folks -- if any come in. You're the folks Bill Gable mentioned, I take it."

Before bedtime six cardboard boxes and a bushel basket had been filled with things to be moved. Mr. Mandelle bought the furniture and the linoleum rugs for twenty-seven dollars and he and Mrs. Bryant traded even for the stoves.

"Is that a lot for our things?" Jody asked as he locked the back door.

"Well," his mother said, "not a lot exactly. But probably as much or more than anyone else'd give us. We bought it all secondhand, except the chest of drawers. And it's cheap."

He was almost asleep when he thought

of a question which had come into his mind earlier. He sat up in bed and listened. Was his mother still up? He heard the rustling of paper and went to the door of the kitchen.

She was copying figures on a piece of paper. She'd rolled her hair up on fat pink curlers. And they bobbed as she looked from one sheet of yellow paper to another.

"What you doing now, Mom?" Jody asked.

"Oh, making lists," she answered. "Here's what we have, and here's what I'd like to buy to spruce up the caboose. And here's what we'll have left if I take one from the other. What's on your mind?"

"I got to thinking," Jody said. "Do you think we can carry all our things over there? Some of the stuff is pretty heavy. Like my beds and the mattresses."

"No, no," his mother said. "I thought you heard. Mr. Mandelle offered to haul some things for us. It's part of the deal, I guess. Anyway, it won't cost us anything."

"That's neat," Jody said. "Well, good night again."

"Good night, Jody," she said. "Now don't you get to worrying about anything else. Just get a good rest."

Jody felt a little guilty after he went to bed. "I really wasn't worried. I just didn't want to carry stuff across the lots. Or have Tony see me going across Walnut Street at the end of a bed. He'd sure say plenty about that."

Somehow Jody felt he should be more worried about the whole thing. He wasn't. Not a bit. The idea of living in the caboose with grass and trees all around seemed like an adventure -- or a summer long game.

"But it's probably not that to Mom. She's out there figuring about the money we have and what we need. And I know she's thinking about whether she can find a job." He went to sleep wondering what he could do to help.

During the next week Jody helped his mother get ready to move the coming

Saturday. Jody would be home then and could help. By Saturday they would have things in order so that the men could move their things without losing too much time.

On Saturday morning he awoke to the sound of men's voices and of something bumping against the wall. His mother came to the door. "You'd better get up! Or the men will be loading you on the truck in your P.J.'s."

Jody couldn't find his clothes. He wasn't wide awake enough to remember that they'd packed everything but one clean outfit. It was in the bathroom.

He had barely time to eat his rolls and drink two glasses of milk. The truck was loaded by the time the sun rose above the low roof of Gable's grocery store.

No one was in sight as Jody climbed on the back of the truck and sat down in his mother's rocking chair. Then he reached out for the picnic basket in which the dishes were packed.

"Are you going to ride back here?"

Jody asked.

"No. I'm going to lock up and walk. I'll carry my lamp. I don't want it broken."

"You can't use it," Jody said.

"I know," his mother said. "But it's so pretty. I love the wild roses on the shade. It seems like I saved trading stamps forever and two days to get it."

The motor started with a chug, then the truck roared down the alley and across Walnut.

Jody had to hold onto the sideboard with one hand as the truck jounced along the cinder drive toward the old factory.

The men had the furniture unloaded by the time Mrs. Bryant reached the caboose. They stayed to put the beds together. For a while Jody thought his bunk wouldn't fit across the end -- that the foot might be stuck part way up one wall. "Maybe I'll have to sleep uphill," he worried.

By ten o'clock the boxes were all unpacked and the caboose began to look like home. The beds were made and the brown spreads made them look like a couch. The clothes were hung behind the curtain at the end. And the glass lamp was placed in the center of the white enameled table.

Jody sat down on the end of a bed and looked around. "It really looks great," he said. "Except for one thing."

"What's that?" his mother asked.

"There's no stove. And I'm starved already," Jody said.

"We'll have it soon," Mrs. Bryant said. "Mr. Mandelle sent word he'd have it fixed up and over here by noon. Think you can make peanut butter do until then?"

7

The owner of the secondhand furniture store brought the stove over at noon. Jody and his mother were ready to eat a cold lunch when the truck came up the drive. Jody stood on the platform and watched as the red pickup snorted and jolted to a stop.

Mr. Mandelle climbed out and looked up at Jody. "That's a pretty high step," he said. "Can't you folks find a box or something around here?"

"There are some pieces of railroad ties over there," Jody said. "But they're pretty heavy."

"Maybe I can budge them," Mr. Mandelle said.

Jody jumped down to help and within a few minutes three square chunks, two in back and one in front made stepping easier.

"Can we help you with the stove?" Mrs. Bryant asked.

"No, no," Mr. Mandelle said. "It doesn't weigh more'n forty pounds. But maybe you'd better cover your eatables. There are likely birds' nests and dust in that chimney pipe."

"We'll take our food out under the trees and get out of your way," Mrs. Bryant said.

"Before you get to enjoying yourself too much," the man said. "Would you bring in the two-gallon can of oil so I can try out the stove?"

After Jody sat down in the wavy grass his mother said, "I hadn't thought about oil. We have some left in the tank at the apartment. But how can we get it out? What in? Cans might cost more than oil."

"Doesn't the big tank belong to us?" Jody asked.

"No. It was there when we moved in."

"I might find some cans or jugs or something on the dump," Jody said. He reached for a second sandwich and looked up to see Carlos coming across the weedy lot. His friend seemed to be leaping like a long-legged rabbit in order to get over the tall weeds.

"Hi," Jody said. "I thought you'd come."

"I wanted to help move," Carlos said as he sat down on the grass. "But I had to watch my little brother while my mamma slept."

"Here, Carlos," Mrs. Bryant said, "have a banana."

"Gracias," Carlos said. "I just ate but it seems like there is always room in me for bananas."

The noon traffic was heavy over on Walnut Street. Tires of cars whirred and long trucks rumbled across the railroad track. But the sounds were far enough away that Jody could hear a singing zinging from somewhere near them.

He looked up through the new leaves. They were still so small that he could see the sky in many places. Like a green umbrella with lots of holes.

"I hear honeybees," Mrs. Bryant said. "Do you suppose this is a bee tree?" She got up and circled the tree. Then she walked to the one at the other end of the caboose. "I was right," she said.

The boys ran to where she stood. Bees were circling and zinging in and out of a hollow in the tall tree.

"That's a sure sign of spring," Jody's mother said.

"Is there honey in there?" Jody asked.

"Some, maybe," his mother answered. "But it's more likely the winter store is about gone. That's why they're out looking for blossoms -- so they can make more."

As they watched, Mr. Mandelle came out of the caboose, wiping his hands on a big red handkerchief. "Well, there you are folks! All set up! Are you sure you know how to light it, ma'am? I had it going just now, but turned it off."

"You'd better show me," Mrs. Bryant said. "This is something I wouldn't want to do by guesswork."

"What you going to do now?" Carlos asked.

"Well, I meant to go over to the dump," Jody said. "And look for cans to hold the oil we have left. Want to go?"

"Sure," Carlos said. "But I think there's a rule about keeping stuff that burns. My dad knows because he works at the station."

"What kind of a rule?" Jody asked.

"I don't know. But we could ask," Carlos said. "My father works today."

"I'll ask Mom," Jody said. "Be right back."

Mrs. Bryant was pouring water into a kettle when Jody walked in. Little drops of moisture hissed as she set the pan over the blue flame.

"What are you going to do now, Mom?" Jody asked.

"I thought I'd scrub the floor first, then me," she answered. "Why?"

"Carlos said his dad might know how we could get the oil over here. Could we go ask him?"

"That'd be fine," his mother said. "I thought we might go over to the shopping center later. I'm going to let loose of a little money. See if Carlos would like to go with us."

"OK, Mom. Be seeing you."

The boys cut across to the cinder drive. This was the long way out to Walnut Street. But there weren't any weeds or sticking nettles to cling to their clothes.

Mr. Mendez was fixing a punctured tire. He listened as Carlos spoke rapidly in Spanish. Then he went inside the office to talk to the manager.

"Doesn't your father speak English?" Jody asked.

"Oh, si," Carlos said. "But slowly. It's easier to explain things in Spanish. And quicker."

Mr. Mendez came from behind the station carrying two red five-gallon cans. "You are permitted to use these," he said. "Then return them."

"Won't you -- or the owner -- need them?" Jody asked.

"No. There are others," Mr. Mendez said. "And when people run out of gasoline they don't want to carry so much. We loan them smaller cans."

"Thank you, Mr. Mendez," Jody said.

As the boys headed toward the apartment, Jody said, "I don't know how to get oil from the big tank to these cans. Who could I ask?"

"Ask me," Carlos said. "It's easy. You use a little hose and do what is called siphoning."

"How do you know this?" Jody asked.

"When you move many times you learn much," Carlos said. "Some bueno things. Some bad."

The boys got one full can of oil and some in the other. "We can take this," Jody said. "I don't know how we'll get the full one over to the caboose."

Jody pulled and Carlos pushed!

"That's easy," Carlos said. "We have a little wagon. It was on the dump and my father fixed the axle."

It took a long time to get the loaded wagon over curbs and up the cinder driveway. Jody pulled and Carlos pushed.

Mrs. Bryant saw them coming from the drive and across the weedy lot. She hurried out to meet them. "My lands alive!" she said. "Such a load! You boys must be worn out."

She set the cans under the caboose and wiped some spilled oil from the bed of the wagon.

"Are you going to the shopping center with us, Carlos?" she asked.

"Oh, I forgot to say anything about it," Jody said. "We've been so busy. Do you suppose you can?"

"I'd better ask," Carlos said. "And find a pair of clean pants."

"I'll go with you," Jody said. "Maybe your mom will let you if I'm there."

Jody's mother smiled. "So that's it! Know your moms pretty well, I see."

72

Mrs. Mendez gave Carlos permission to go with the Bryants. But she told him to be sure to be back before the sun went down. "So many bad things happen in dark places," she said. "I would not want you to be hurt, or have others think you were with those who caused trouble."

"What did she mean?" Jody asked as the boys thumped down the shaky wooden steps on the back of the old house.

"A lot of stuff's been happening," Carlos said. "The whirling red lights of police cars can be seen on the side streets almost every night."

"You mean fights?" Jody asked.

"Sometimes," Carlos said. "And other things, like stealing and tearing up stuff."

Jody was about ready to ask if his friend knew who was causing all the trouble when Carlos grabbed his arm.

"Let's cut across this yard. Tony's up in front of the laundromat."

Jody didn't argue. He just followed. But he couldn't help wondering. Why was Carlos ducking Tony? Oh, he knew there were plenty of reasons guys didn't run to meet him. "And I'm one who does not," Jody realized. "But I don't hide."

He was about to ask if his friend had had a fight with Tony. The words were ready to pop out. Then Carlos said, "I'm sorry, amigo. I didn't know Tony was close enough to hear."

"Hear what?"

"When I was coming over to see you I called to my mamma from the bottom of the steps, 'Could I go to the caboose and see Jody?' And Tony and Tim and some other kid were coming down the alley."

"So they said a lot of things. Made fun," Jody said.

"Not Tim," Carlos answered. "He only stood there. And the other one probably doesn't know you. I didn't know him. You want to know what Tony said?"

Jody shrugged his shoulders. "No. Anyway, I can guess."

"I'm sorry."

"Oh, forget about it," Jody said. "He had to know sometime. You can't exactly hide a caboose. Let's hurry."

It was ten blocks from the caboose to the shopping center and no buses ran out that far. Mrs. Bryant asked Carlos if she could borrow his wagon. "I'm going to get some bulky things. And our arms would be numb by the time we get home."

She looked at Jody's face and smiled. "Don't worry. I'll pull it! If you're all at once too grown up to be tugging a toy."

"It's not that," Jody said. But it was and he knew it. He couldn't understand why something which seemed great just a year or two ago wasn't right now. What happened to change things -- or how he felt?

"Today the wagon is not a toy," Carlos said. "It is a shopping cart. Yes?"

"Sure," Jody said. "Let's go."

Mrs. Bryant bought the items she had on the list she'd made the night before. The first stop was at the dollar store where she picked out two rolls of thin carpeting. "It will cover most of our floor," she said. "And we can take it up easily to clean it. I think it'll look real homey."

The next stop was at the supermarket. She asked the boys if they'd wait outside with the wagon. "Then I'll give you a quarter apiece to spend while I go to the hardware store. I wish it were more. You've been such a great help."

"What are you going to get at a hardware store?" Jody asked.

His mother smiled and said, "I have to buy a coal oil lamp for one thing. And maybe nothing else. I have to see how much something costs first. I'll tell you later."

After the heavy brown sack of groceries was stashed between the two rolls of carpet the boys ran around the L-shaped walk to the variety store. Carlos bought a comic book, a dime bag of marbles and four balls of bubble gum. "I'll divide the marbles and the gum with my brother," he said. "I hope he's big enough to know which round ball to put in his mouth."

Jody bought a kite and a ball of string. There was plenty of room around the caboose for a shield-shaped kite to soar and dip and sail into the sky.

When they met Mrs. Bryant and told her what they'd bought, she smiled. "Marbles and kites. It's really spring. At least I hope so."

"Did you get whatever it was you wanted in there?" Jody asked.

"Yes. I did," his mother said and let him peek into the gray bag.

"Paint," Jody said. "I thought Mr. Gable was going — "

"To give us blue paint for the caboose," his mother said. "You're right, and he is. But this is brass, or a kind of goldlike color."

She talked as they walked. A long time ago her grandfather had taken her to the Big Four station when someone important was making a trip across the state and making a brief stop in Fort Jefferson. "It might even have been the President of the United States. I truly don't remember," she said. "But I'll never forget that railroad car. It was new and clean, the color of my grandmother's polished rosewood piano. And the railing on the back platform was shining. It was early morning. And the sun made it look like gold."

"So you're going to paint the miniporch that color," Jody said.

"I am," his mother answered. "A blue caboose with a golden brass porch. The words sound pretty."

"And they make a bueno picture, Mrs. Bryant," Carlos said.

The sun was still above the rooftops when they got back to their new home. Carlos hurried on across the lots toward Walnut Street.

Jody's mother put the groceries away and spread the strips of carpet while he tore an old skirt into pieces. Then he tied them to make a tail for the kite.

"Could I see if it will fly, Mom?" he asked. "Will there be time before dark?"

"I think so. I'll come out with you. It's been a busy day and I could do with a little rest."

They walked over to the cinder drive. It would be easier to run on it, and if the kite fell on the weeds in the lot the bright yellow paper would be torn. Jody made several tries before the evening breeze lifted and carried the kite into the sky. Once it was up on the air current it floated and turned with the red tail curling and uncurling behind it. A kite was a free thing.

"A kite is a free thing."

Jody and his mother sat down in the grass at the edge of the drive. The wind-carried kite gave little tugs on the string which was wrapped around Jody's hand.

"It looks pretty," Jody's mother said. "Like a big yellow butterfly."

"Butterflies don't have tails," Jody said. "Not red ones or any kind."

"Listen," Jody's mother said. "I think I heard church bells."

"There is one. A new one. Over back of the shopping center," Jody said. "Carlos saw the steeple. It's like a gold finger pointing up."

"I think I'll look into this. Find out what time they have services," his mother said. "I always went regular at home. I shouldn't have let anyone throw me off that track."

Jody grinned. He felt good. Tired but good. "Well, Mom. You're really on the track now. Living in the end of a train."

9

Jody sat on the steps of the mini-porch while his mother toasted cheese sandwiches and made hot chocolate. Soft sounds were all around him. A bird twittered in one tree. And one answered from the other. He could hear the faint hiss and sputter of the flame of the oil stove. Walnut Street and Tony and trouble seemed far away -- much farther than four blocks.

His mother came to the door. "Will you please run over to the hydrant and get a bucket of water?" she asked. "Then we'll eat."

The caboose looked like a real home to Jody when he came back. The tall clear chimney of the lamp threw a circle of gold light over one end. The new strips of carpet covered most of the floor. It felt soft to Jody's feet. Not like the slick linoleum in the apartment.

"You scrub up while I brown the other side of these sandwiches," his mother said. "This stove works real well."

They ate without saying much. Both were tired. It seemed to be a time for soaking up the stillness.

As Mrs. Bryant rose from the table she said, "There's one thing I wish I'd priced this afternoon. Curtain material. It wouldn't take much. And curtains soften a room."

"We can go back tomorrow -- after school," Jody said.

"Well, we'll see. I want to get the paint and start on that in the morning."

Jody started to lie down then he remembered his kite. He'd left it outside; and it might rain.

He hurried out and folded the tail into loops and untied the string from the balsa wood sticks.

"Where could I keep my kite, Mom?" he called.

"Oh, under the bed," his mother answered. "My grandmother always said a wide bedspread could hide a multitude of things. I'll get some flat boxes for storage from Mr. Gable's grocery."

Jody suddenly thought of his homework. He could hardly stay awake as he multiplied fractions. He needed props for his eyelids.

Before the problems on the last row were solved the wind began to rise. The branches of the trees swished and the small tin chimney squeaked a little.

"We may be in for a storm," Mrs. Bryant said.

"We're safe here, aren't we?" Jody asked.

"Yes," his mother said. "This caboose has been here a long time and had many a chance to blow away."

Jody saw a flash of light outside one of the west windows. At first he thought it was lightning. Then a car door slammed. Within a couple of minutes he heard Mr. Gable say, "Anyone at home in there?"

"Yes, sir," Mrs. Bryant answered. "Come in."

"Well, I brought these cans of paint. I'll set them down out here first."

"Will the rain hurt them -- if it comes?" Mrs. Bryant asked.

"It's coming," Mr. Gable answered. "but these cans are sealed tight."

The tall man had to duck his head to get in the door. He stood still and looked around. "I wouldn't have believed this place could look so good," he said. "You two sure have used a lot of elbow grease these past two days."

"What does he mean?" Jody wondered. "What's elbow grease? I'll ask Mom."

Mr. Gable was about to leave when he stopped and scratched his head. "I just about forgot half of what I came for. And my wife would send me right back over here. She really got after me for not telling you more about the job I have in mind. But I don't dare let it be known there's an opening anywhere. Or I'd be pestered with people applying."

"I understand that," Jody's mother said. "With so many people out of work."

"Well, you stop by when you finish our dusting and sweeping. By then I'll have things lined up," Mr. Gable said.

"I wonder what he means," Jody's mother said as she shut the back door. The wind was making the fan-shaped flame of the lamp waver and flicker.

"He said it was something about a job," Jody said.

"I know," his mother answered. "But where? Doing what? Oh, well, I'll find out in the morning."

"I thought you were going to paint," Jody said.

"I was. But this is more important. First things first," she said.

By this time raindrops were pattering on the roof of the caboose. Mrs. Bryant shut the east windows. The air was fresh and the sound of the shower made Jody sleepy. "I think I'll go to bed," he said.

"It's time," his mother answered. "And I'll do the same as soon as I shine up this stove a little."

The rain kept on. It seemed to be floating Jody into sleep. He turned over to keep the light out of his eyes, and hit one elbow against the wall. "Hey, Mom," he said. "What's elbow grease?"

His mother was down on her knees rubbing the gray enamel jacket of the stove with a soft cloth.

"It's what I'm using now," she said, "my hands and arms. Or in other words -- work. What did you think it was, soap or scouring powder?"

"I guess," Jody said. "Good night."

It seemed that he'd just closed his eyes when his mother called, "It's Monday morning. Time to begin another week."

She made Jody's bed while he ate and they walked down the cinder drive together. The weeds and the grass were wet with the rain of the night before.

"Will you be home when I get there?" Jody asked as they came to the place where he'd branch off to go to Riley School.

"I'm not sure," his mother said. "Maybe. You'd better check with Mr. Gable before you go home. I'll leave word there."

Jody reached the school earlier than usual. He'd given himself plenty of time, not knowing how much longer it took to walk seven blocks than it did to go four.

The janitor was unlocking the doors. No one Jody knew was in sight. The truck which hauled milk to the cafeteria was backing up to the end of the walk.

The building seemed different when the halls were empty. Jody's steps sounded loud, like he was walking in a hollow place.

Miss McKee, his homeroom teacher, was watering the grapefruit and avocado plants. This was one of the class science projects.

"You're early, Jody," the teacher said.

"Yes'm. We moved and I didn't know how long it would take to get here."

"Where do you live now?" Miss McKee asked.

A strange thing happened to Jody. He began to pour out words about the caboose even while he was thinking maybe Miss McKee would think there was something wrong about living in such a place. It was like his mind was running on a double track.

"We're going to paint the caboose blue," he finished. "And the railing on the end will be kind of gold."

"Oh, Jody," the teacher said. "This sounds exciting. Like a real adventure."

Jody looked straight at Miss McKee. She meant it. She wasn't faking. He felt good.

"Your mother sounds like a wonderful person," the teacher said.

These words made him feel even better.

10

Jody started toward his seat. He had a library book which was due. He wanted to get another one to take home. Maybe two or three. "I'll have more time to read over there," he thought.

There was more noise in the halls as Jody came to the short flight of steps that led to the library. The sound of many voices was kind of like music out of tune. Especially one. Jody was able to hear Tony above all the others. "No wonder," Jody thought. "He wants me to hear."

Jody turned a little sideways and caught a glimpse of Tim and Tony and two other boys. They were standing at the end of the hall which led to their fifth-grade room.

When Tony saw that Jody was looking his way, he raised one fist up and down in the air and said, "Toot! Toot," again, loud enough so it could be heard above moving feet and the hum of voices.

"So that's how he's going to act," Jody thought. "Just like he always does. Making fun. Putting people down." His face felt hot clear back to his ears. He looked around. No one seemed to be paying much attention to Tony. They were going on about what they had to do. "And I should do the same," Jody decided. "Before the bell rings."

He tried not to look toward Tony's desk. This wasn't easy because it was straight across the room, two rows away. And he kept shoving the dread of noon hour to the back of his mind. Tony did a lot of things besides making fun of people, when there were no teachers in sight. Things like starting fights and writing junky things on walls and even stealing from lockers. Teachers would really have to have eyes in the back of their heads to keep track of all that guys like Tony did.

Jody was glad he didn't eat with Tony in the cafeteria. They were assigned seats at different tables. Carlos was almost back to back with Jody.

"What are you going to do this noon?" Carlos asked.

"Oh, I don't know," Jody said. Then he lowered his voice. "I feel like going to the room and hiding. Running like a chicken."

"On account of Tony?" Carlos asked. "I heard him! Don't worry, amigo! I'll stick by you."

The sunshine was like bright silver when the boys walked out the wide front doors. They blinked their eyes several times.

"Want to play basketball?" Carlos asked.

Jody looked toward the paved court. "It's pretty crowded. We'd probably get our hands on a ball about twice!"

"I brought some marbles," Carlos said. "Want to play?"

The game of marbles was kid stuff to most fifth-graders. Jody knew this. But he still liked to play. And anyway, who passed a law saying a guy was too old to play when he was eleven?

With a sharp stone Carlos marked a circle in a bare place near the school building. Jody liked the look of the bright colors mingled with the milky glass. And the clicks of the marbles against each others were like a little song.

Suddenly a shadow fell across the ring. Then a foot shoved the marbles to one side. Jody didn't have to look up to see who was standing behind him. He'd have known if he hadn't heard the screechy voice saying, "Toot, toot!"

Tony wasn't alone. He never was when he was doing his mean things. He needed people to back him up. Like Tim and the Corbette twins who were laughing like crazy now.

As Jody started to get up he glanced

"Toot, toot yourself!" said Jody!

at Carlos. His friend's brown eyes seemed to have sparks of fire in them. "He's ready to fight for me," Jody realized.

Jody wanted to crawl away or get up on his feet and run. But where could he go that Tony or his voice wouldn't follow?

So he handed the five marbles across the circle to Carlos and stood up. He felt trembly inside as he turned to face the boys who stood behind him. He felt like socking Tony. But fighting was no way of settling things. Guys just got madder.

He really didn't know what to say either. No one could outtalk or outyell Tony. Then an idea popped into Jody's mind. He looked straight at Tony, grinned, and put a doubled-up fist in the air. As he pumped his hand up and down, he said, "Toot, toot!"

An odd look came over Tony's face. "He doesn't know what to do," Jody thought. He glanced at Tim who was looking down and digging the toe of one sneaker into the dirt. The Corbette twins turned and walked away. Then Tim, and last of all Tony, followed.

Carlos thumped Jody's back. "Bueno, amigo! That was a fine way to stop that mouth of Tony's. I was ready to do it with my fist."

"I know," Jody said. "I didn't want you to get in trouble because of me. Hey! Maybe we've got enough recess to finish this game -- if you give me back the five marbles."

There wasn't much time to think about Tony or the caboose or anything but schoolwork that afternoon. During science class the fifth grade was given a test covering the past six weeks. And the last period was given over to special projects.

Jody was making a model of a cone volcano with clay and other things. He used bits of green sponge for trees, and chunks of wood painted with watercolors for houses in the valley.

Carlos came to Jody's room to borrow a stapler for his teacher. He stopped at the worktable to watch him work. "I thought volcanoes tore things up," he said. "Here everything's green and neat."

"Some volcanoes are what they call dormant," Jody said. "That's like sleeping. They smoke a little but don't erupt."

"How are you going to make yours smoke?" Carlos asked.

Jody grinned. "Miss McKee figured that out. Look down inside. See that little can? With foil on the inside?"

"Sure. What's it for?"

"Watch." Jody picked up a small square of something which looked like charcoal. He went to the teacher's desk and she came back, lit the square with a match, and dropped it to the inside of the volcano. Pale gray smoke curled into the air. It smelled a little like flowers.

"What is that stuff?" Carlos asked.

"It's incense," Jody said.

"Volcanoes don't really smell good, do they?" Carlos asked.

"No. But it'd be nice if they did," the teacher said.

Carlos was waiting at the end of the

walk when school was out. The boys walked to Gable's store together. Jody had to wait awhile before the owner had time to talk to him. Kids from Riley Elementary and Blaine Junior High rushed in after school. It took as long sometimes to sell one jelly doughnut, three sticks of bubble gum, or a dime candy bar as it did to check out a big sack of groceries. Kids who had only a few cents to spend had a hard time making up their minds.

When everyone had gone except two little girls Mr. Gable looked over the candy case and asked, "You wanting to know about your mamma, Jody?"

"Yes. Mom told me to ask you."

"Well, she's at the caboose now. Probably painting. Or finishing up," Mr. Gable said. "This time tomorrow evening she'll like as not be at the laundromat."

That meant she had another job. Jody couldn't wait to get home to find out more. But he did remember to say, "Thank you, sir," before he said, "Come on, Carlos," and hurried out the door.

Jody saw his mother come down the steps of the mini-porch as he trotted across the lots. The weeds didn't bother him so much now. He was making a path.

As he came closer he saw that his mother was washing her hands. Then his nose told him she wasn't using water. It was the fuel oil they used in the stove.

"Hey, Mom," Jody called. "What are you doing anyhow?"

His mother arose from the stooping position, holding her hands over a small white basin. "I'm scrubbing paint specks off me," she said. "If I don't, people can see for days what color I've been using."

"You quitting for today?" Jody asked.

"I'm done," his mother said. "On the inside, that is."

"You are! You must have worked awful fast."

"Not really," his mother said. "The boards have been stained before -- a long time ago. And they're pretty smooth. Of course it may need a second coat. I can tell better when it dries."

"Can I go in?" Jody asked. "Will it rub off?"

"Go on. Just don't lean on anything for an hour or so."

Jody whistled as he looked at his mother's work. "It's a real room now. Not just an old forsaken caboose."

His mother came to the door and stood behind him. "Like it?" she asked.

"I think it's neat!" Jody said.

"Well, so do I," his mother answered. "But I've got news I'm just jumping to tell."

"You got a job. Right?" Jody said.

"Did Mr. Gable tell you?"

"No. Not exactly. But from what he said I guessed."

"Well sit down while I get the oil smell off my hands and I'll tell you."

She began with her visit to the store owner's wife. Mrs. Gable said her sister wanted someone to do cleaning for two hours two mornings a week. Then Mr. Gable had at least four hours of work in the laundromat every afternoon.

"The pay's pretty good," Mrs. Bryant said. "Not as much as if I went to a factory. But there's no bus fare and probably no layoffs, if I do a good job. And I'll be close enough to keep tabs on you!" she said.

Jody liked that. He wanted to know where she was too. In case he needed to ask something. Or tell her good things. He wasn't used to having his dad around. Or going to him with problems. Or anything. But with Mom it was different.

"I think I'll hang the curtain over our

closet-dressing room," Mrs. Bryant said. "I painted that end first. Maybe you could hang the clothes while I do that."

Within twenty minutes the caboose was in good order again. Jody's mother said she wanted to go over to the shopping center. "Even if I am tired."

"Could I go for you?" Jody asked.

"For the screen wire for the windows you'd be fine," his mother said. "But now that I know we're going to have an income I'm going to go ahead and buy curtain material. Something white and thin."

"Well, I wouldn't know where to look or what to buy. And maybe I'd better stay here. Carlos might come over."

After his mother changed clothes and started out the door she turned. "Did you see the lawn mower?"

"No -- where'd it come from?" Jody asked.

"Mr. Gable had it sharpened," Mrs. Bryant said. "He doesn't use this one since he bought a power mower. I pushed it over when I came home this morning."

"I think I'll try it out," Jody said.

"Good," his mother said. "You do that. And I'll buy stuff to make your favorite food for supper."

"Oh, man! Cheeseburgers!" Jody said as he followed his mother down the steps.

The grass around the caboose was thick and fairly high. But the mower was sharp and well oiled. The blades whirred, and clattered a little, as they clipped a path. Jody marked off a strip on the side of the caboose that faced the street four blocks away. "This is the part we see when we come home," he thought.

His arms ached by the time he'd made five rounds. But when he stepped back and looked at what was done he wanted to go on. The mown part looked smooth like the yards over on Twelfth Street and the grass in Rose Park. Not bare and trashy like those over around the apartment.

Suddenly Jody realized that he was

nearly starved. He'd been so interested in his mother's news that he hadn't thought of eating when he got home from school. This didn't happen often.

He ran inside and spread peanut butter on one slice of bread and sprinkled brown sugar over it. He pressed down gently on the top slice so sugar sprinkles wouldn't fall on the clean floor.

As he went back toward the mower he saw a white panel truck coming along the cinder drive from the direction of Walnut Street. Jody watched, wondering who could be coming to see him or his mother.

But the truck curved on around toward the front of the old factory. Two men got out and went inside. One was all dressed up, except for one funny thing. He had his collar on backward.

The men didn't seem to notice Jody. He went on with his mowing but a lot of questions whirred around in his mind. Who were they? What were they doing? Had Mr. Gable sold the factory? Would anyone else want us to live in the caboose?

The men left before Jody's mother came back from the shopping center. He wanted to tell her about the men and see how she felt. "Or do I just want to hear her say there's nothing for us to worry about?" he wondered.

But his mother was so excited and happy that he just couldn't say anything that might spoil things for her.

"You've surely worked hard, Jody," she said as she stopped at the steps. "I bet you're hungry."

"Well, I fixed a peanut-butter sandwich," Jody said.

"That won't fill you up. I'll hurry and get this meat made into patties and fried."

Jody had his patch of yard cut before he was called in to eat. As he wheeled the mower to the back of the caboose, he decided to cut another section the next night. In four nights they'd have a yard all around them.

"Carlos didn't come?" Jody's mother asked as he washed his hands.

"No. He probably had to do something. Like watch his brother."

"How was school today?" Jody's mother asked as they sat down to eat.

"Oh, great," Jody said. He thought of Tony and his tooting. But he didn't tell that. He really didn't understand why. Usually he ran home letting off steam about things -- some not as big as this. "But I guess I don't want to worry Mom. Or make her think there's something to be ashamed of in living in a caboose. She's worked so hard. Now, I'm protecting her," he thought.

So he told her about the volcano and its sweet-smelling smoke and the library books and how interested the teacher was in where they were living. These things made his mom feel good.

Jody did his homework while his mother did the dishes. Then he read while she sewed on her curtains. The circle of golden light from the lamp was wide enough to include them both. His mother's rocking chair squeaked a little, like a cheerful cricket. And the blue flame of the oil stove drove the chill out of the caboose.

12

Jody almost forgot about seeing the men go into the old factory until the next evening. He'd gone to the laundromat to find out what time his mother would be home.

She was polishing the pale green washers which were not in use. Water swished in the others. The big drums of the dryers went around and around, tumbling clothes. The place was filled with steam and the lemony smell of soap.

"You about ready to go home?" Jody asked.

"Well, my time's up in fifteen minutes,"

she said. "But things are sort of in a mess here. I'd like to scrub the floor before going home. Want to wait?"

"No. Carlos is going to see if he can come over. He wants to help me mow."

"That's nice," Mrs. Bryant said. "Let me get my purse and give you a couple of dimes. Get yourselves ice-cream bars or something."

As the boys crossed the lots on Jody's path the white panel truck came down the drive.

"Who's that?" Carlos asked.

"I don't know," Jody said. "I saw some guys over here yesterday."

The boys mowed at both ends of the caboose home. But they couldn't get to the grass in the tracks.

"That scraggly stuff spoils the looks of things," Jody said. "What can we do about it?"

"Well, we could pull it up with our hands," Carlos said. "But it's pretty tough."

"Yeah. And it would keep growing

back," Jody said.

"If we had dirt we could cover the track and plant flowers," Carlos said. "Like red or yellow. They'd be bueno next to a blue caboose."

"That's a keen idea," Jody said. "And I know where there's a whole big pile of dirt. Out behind the factory."

"Why is it there?" Carlos . asked. "Could we get some?"

"I don't know," Jody said. "But we can ask Mr. Gable."

Before the week was over the boys had hauled dozens of loads of black mealy soil in the little wagon Mr. Mendez had found on the dump. Mr. Gable had given them permission to take some of the dirt from the big pile from behind the factory.

"It's been there since the county dug the drainage ditch across my property. And no improvement's a bad idea. No matter what the future has in store."

"What does he mean by that?" Jody wondered. "Good or bad?"

Jody's mother was excited about the

idea of having flower beds in their yard. "I'll have to think about what kind of seeds to buy," she said. "Things that will grow fast and bloom a lot. Then we'll go to the shopping center Saturday night. When I get off work. After I get paid."

"We could wait and go Sunday," Jody said. "Then we'd have more time."

"No. We're going to church Sunday," Mrs. Bryant said.

They were sitting at the table when she said this. They'd finished eating the thick potato soup, canned peaches, and cookies. The flame of the coal oil lamp wavered a little in the evening breeze. It was so warm they didn't need to burn the heating part of the stove.

"Do you know anyone over at that church?" Jody asked.

"Well, I won't know until we get there," his mother said. "Why? Does it bother you to go where everyone might be strangers to us?"

"A little," Jody said. He remembered

how we felt the first day at Riley School. Like everyone was looking at him. In a way it was like a bad dream he had sometimes. In these nightmares he went to school barefoot and tried to hide all day long, behind coats in the halls and in the cupboard where the teacher kept paper and chalk and the extra erasers.

"Well, I guess I'll be a little uneasy too," his mother said. "But after the first time it'll be better."

"You think we'll keep on going?" Jody asked. He didn't know if this was something he'd want to do a lot or not. He couldn't really remember much about how it was.

"I think so," his mother said. She went on talking while she did the dishes and sat down in her rocker to finish hemming the white curtains. She told Jody some things he had heard before, but now she added to it. She finished by saying, "It's hard to explain but I liked the way church made me feel. Maybe it was the music. Or the Bible lesson or the friendliness. Or all of it together. Of course everyone there had lived close together for years and years. In this new place there'll be no one we know at first. And besides, some of your school friends could go to this church."

"I sure hope it's not Tony," Jody thought.

Jody finished his homework and read in one of his library books until his eyelids got heavy. It was a story about Harriett Tubman. She led a lot of slaves to safety over something called the underground railroad. The author made Jody feel like he was there.

He was on the last chapter when his mother said, "I think I'll get some sleep. I want to get up at daylight tomorrow."

"Daylight," Jody said. "Why so early?"

"Oh, I thought I told you," she said. "I'm going to begin painting the outside of the caboose. I should get one side done a day."

"Why couldn't I help?" Jody asked.

"No reason why not," his mother said. "We have two brushes. But you'd have to quit in time to get scrubbed for school. And you need to get to sleep now."

Before Sunday morning the caboose was blue inside and out. Even the railing on the platform was painted. Jody's mother finished it up just before darkness came Saturday night. "I can't wait to see how that golden brass will show up in the sunshine," she said. "But I'll have to, won't I?"

They made the trip to the shopping center when she got off at four. Jody mowed the front section of the yard for the second time. He also smoothed the dirt in the track flower beds. Mr. Gable loaned them a bamboo rake.

His mother bought six packets of flower seeds, two each of California poppies, bachelor's buttons, and zinnias. "Mrs. Gable says these bloom for a long time. And that's what we need."

They slept until nearly eight o'clock the next morning. They'd worked hard all week and Jody would have liked to have stayed in bed a lot longer. Going to church didn't seem to be a good idea at all.

Mrs. Bryant said, "It's a good thing my job is at a laundromat. I don't know how I'd get clothes ironed over here where there's no electricity."

"Do you miss it a lot?" Jody asked.

"Not so much as I thought," she answered. "Of course I grew up on a farm where we heated irons on a stove. But that was a long time ago. The thing I miss most is a way to keep things cold."

She bought Jody a red bow tie to wear with his white dress-up shirt. And she wore a flowered dress she hadn't had on for more than a year. "Not been many places lately," she said.

As they walked down the steps of the mini-porch she touched the gleaming railing. "It's dry." They walked down the cinder drive, then turned to look back. The blue caboose was a pretty sight. The railing shone like gold in the morning sun. The grass was green and white clouds, which were like cotton, drifted across the sky.

Jody felt good. Maybe church wouldn't be so bad.

He heard music as they walked in the wide doors. The place seemed cool and a little dark. Light came in through windows made of bits of colored glass. The pieces made pictures.

His mother led the way to a seat near the back. Jody looked down at first, feeling embarrassed or bashful or something. Then he began to look around. He saw a girl who was in his class at school. And the other fifth-grade teacher was across the aisle. So everyone was not a stranger.

The music stopped and a man came in from a little door on the side. He walked to a high kind of desk on the platform. Jody had the feeling that he'd seen the man before. Something about him looked familiar. Then he remembered. He was the guy from the factory. The one with the funny collar.

13

After church was over five or six people came up and told Jody's mother their names. Some said they were glad they came, and hoped they'd come back. The minister shook hands with them like he did everyone else.

"And where do you live?" he asked.

Mrs. Bryant smiled and said. "I don't exactly know what our address is yet. You see, sir, we're living in a caboose over -- "

"So you're the ones!" the minister said. "I've been over that way a few times lately. I have watched the improvements appear and I almost envy you."

"You do?" Jody's mother said.

"Yes. It's so quiet and I guess the pioneer or roving spirit in me makes living in such a place seem like an adventure. I'll be over to see you soon."

Jody's feelings were mixed. He liked what the man said about the caboose. But he was uneasy about him and the other men being around the factory. He couldn't help wondering why the minister was coming to see them.

It was nearly one o'clock in the afternoon by the time they got home. They didn't hurry. The sun was warm and the world looked, felt, and even smelled good.

Lilacs were in bloom in one yard, and Jody saw a cardinal and a blue jay before they got home.

"I think I'll fly my kite," he said. "I wish Carlos would come over."

"Why don't you run over and ask him to eat with us?" his mother said. "I have enough ham and it's easy to add another potato or two."

"Maybe he's already eaten," Jody said.

"Well, you can find out. There's time."

Jody hurried to the old neighborhood. He liked the idea of having company for a meal. They hadn't done that for a long time. Not since his dad had come home from Vietnam.

He wondered about his father as he crossed Walnut Street. Where was he and what was he doing? Was it wrong to sort of wish he wouldn't come back? At least until he became like he used to be?

Jody could remember a lot of good things about his father. More good than bad -- before he went to the war.

Carlos was sitting on the steps which led up to the apartment. "My mom wants you to come eat with us," Jody said. "Or have you already?"

"No. My mother worked last night. I just woke her. Wait until I ask."

In a couple of minutes Carlos came downstairs pulling a clean T-shirt over his head.

"My papa and mamma are going to

look for a new place to live, but I'd rather go with you," he said.

"Are you going to move?" Jody asked. He didn't like to think Carlos wouldn't be around. But he could see that the Mendez family would like to be out of the one-room apartment before hot weather came.

"Si," Carlos said. "My papa begins on a steady job Monday. Out at the canning factory."

"Will you move out there? Jody asked.

"My mamma hopes not," Carlos said. "She thinks I've changed schools too many times. She said she has another idea in her mind."

After dinner the boys flew the kite and then they explored the old factory for about the fortieth time.

When the boys returned from the factory Jody's mother was sitting outside under the maple tree. "I just dragged my rocker out and am plain doing nothing for a while," she said.

The boys were lying on their backs

staring up at the branches, when Mrs. Bryant said, "Someone's coming. A boy."

Jody sat up and saw Tim coming slowly across the lot. He was alone. This was unusual. He had been Tony's shadow for months.

"Hi, you guys," Tim said, stopping at the edge of the drive.

"Hi," Jody said.

"Ask him over," his mother whispered. "Where are your manners?"

Jody wasn't at all sure he wanted Tim to see the caboose. He could be here just to find out stuff to tell Tony. So he could make more smart remarks. But he said, "You might as well come on over."

Tim sat down on the grass but his eyes were on the blue caboose. "That sure looks a lot different than it used to," he said.

"Well, we spruced it up a little," Mrs. Bryant said. "Want to see the inside?"

"Why -- sure. I'd like to," Tim said.

There was no way Jody could get out of taking Tim up the steps. But he did motion for Carlos to come along. Tim might have less to say in front of two.

The room looked even nicer than usual to Jody. The thin white curtains sort of danced in the breeze. His mother had spread a white cloth on the table and put her pretty lamp in the center.

Tim whistled. "This is even better than my uncle's big camper," he said. "And I thought it was great. There's a lot more room in here." Tim was first going down the steps. He turned and said, "I wouldn't have blamed you if you told me to mind my own business. After the way I laughed when old Tony made fun."

Jody didn't know what to say. He couldn't tell Tim, "Oh, that's all right!" Because it wasn't.

"He was wrong," Tim said. "This place is neat. Better'n where I live. Maybe I've let him lead me around by the end of my nose too long."

Now Jody did know what to say. Tim sounded like the guy he used to be -- a good friend.

122

"Stick around a while," Jody said. "We might knock a few flies. My baseball's a little lopsided but maybe you guys can hit it, with a lot of practice."

The three boys played in the cinder drive until a car came around the bend. The Mendez family was back from their house hunting and had come to pick up Carlos.

Jody's mother hurried over to the car and asked them to get out and stay for a while.

Mrs. Mendez was shy and started to shake her head. Then Mrs. Bryant said, "I want you to see inside the caboose. And your little boy might like to play on the grass."

"Well, for a little while," Mrs. Mendez said. "I was wondering how much room you have. And how you feel about living in a small place."

The ladies went inside while Mr. Mendez walked to the space on the other side of the factory. Then everyone sat in the grass and talked until it was time for Mr. Mendez to go to the filling station. "This is my last night on that job. I could just not show up. But the owner has been good to me."

Tim rode home with Carlos' family. As the car disappeared Jody's mother said, "Well, we're going to have neighbors."

"What does she mean?" Jody thought. "Who? Does this have anything to do with the men being over at the factory?"

"Mrs. Mendez told me," Jody's mother said. "They've bought a small mobile home and Mr. Gable has rented them a space over on the other side of the drive."

"Great!" Jody said. "Carlos will like that. He didn't want to change schools again."

"And how about you? Will you like having someone near?"

"I sure will," Jody said. "I'll help Carlos mow his yard."

But he thought. "Maybe there's nothing to worry about after all. Mr. Gable surely wouldn't rent space for a mobile home if he was selling this land."

14

The next morning Carlos was waiting for Jody at the end of the walk which led up to James Whitcomb Riley School. He was so excited that he used several Spanish words Jody didn't understand. But he knew what he was saying anyway.

Carlos told about the mobile home and where it was to be parked. Jody didn't let on that he already knew. That would spoil his friend's fun. But he did ask. "When are you going to move?"

"Maybe tonight," Carlos said. "I don't know. I'm supposed to hurry home right after school. Want to come along?"

Jody started to say "yes." Then he remembered. "I have to go home and put an extra coat of paint on the door. Some of the rustiness is showing through."

"OK," Carlos said. But if we do move I'll be seeing you."

Jody stopped by the laundromat after school. "Want me to get something from the grocery?" he asked.

"No. You carry this box of clean ironed clothes and I'll do the food-buying," she said. "I may stick in a surprise or two."

After Jody changed clothes he went outside and began stirring the leftover paint with a flat stick. Then he heard hammering. He stopped to listen. It was coming from inside the factory. That was funny. He hadn't seen a truck this time.

He walked around to the back of the caboose. From there he could see the same white panel truck parked by a side door. As he looked he heard the humming buzz of a saw. He shook his head and went back to work.

He had the painting half done when a

bright orange truck came up the drive. There sure was a lot of traffic around here tonight. This truck had ladders on the side and big coils of wire in the open bed.

By the time the painting was finished Jody was getting more and more curious. His mother was late. He was ready to talk to her about what was going on. He'd kept what he'd seen and heard to himself long enough. Being worried all by himself was lonely.

He scrubbed his hands and walked to the edge of the drive. One man was on the light pole in front of the factory. The other was pulling wire toward the caboose. Both wore metal hats, bright orange, like the truck.

The man on the ground saw Jody. "We'll soon have you hooked up, boy."

Hooked up? They were from the light company. Did Mom know?

He had decided to run back to the laundromat and tell the news when he heard a motor chuffing around the end of the drive. Maybe it could be someone bringing the Mendez mobile home.

As he watched the truck from the secondhand store cut across the grass toward the caboose. The driver gave three quick toots on the horn. And an arm was waving out the open window. It was his mother.

She jumped out of the truck and came toward Jody. "I hitched a ride. Rode with our new-to-us refrigerator."

"Refrigerator!" Jody said. "Did you know we were going to get electricity?"

"No. Not until today," she said. "I'd have told you. Things really happened fast. I'll tell you after I show the man where to put our electric icebox. It's not very big. Like the ones they use in campers. But we don't have room for a regular-size refrigerator.

By the time the small chest-type appliance was in place the electric line had been hooked to the caboose. One of the men came to the door. "You've got juice now, ma'am, if you want to plug stuff in."

"Plug in to what?" Jody asked.

"Didn't you notice? Mr. Gable had his brother-in-law come over and run this strip along one side. The caboose isn't wired. But the strip plugs in to this one outlet under the window. Watch."

She took her lamp with the wild roses on the shade from the shelf above the stove. She connected it with one of the sockets on the strip. The roses seemed to bloom in the light. Next she plugged the refrigerator and its motor clicked, then purred.

"If I'd known for sure the line was to be hooked up, I'd have brought ice cream. That was to be my surprise."

"I could go get it," Jody said.

"Well all right! You do that. And get a pint of cottage cheese too. I'll cook us a few bites -- and put away our clean clothes."

Jody met Tim as he went into the store. He was alone. Tony wasn't in sight. "What are you doing?" Jody asked.

"Oh, nothing much," Tim said.

"Why don't you come over after a while? We could play ball or something." He went on to say that the Mendez family could be moving into their mobile home later in the evening.

"I saw Carlos carrying stuff downstairs," Tim said. "That's why. I'll see if I can help. Then maybe I'll come."

As Jody and his mother ate their crusty fried potatoes and cottage cheese she filled him in on the news.

The minister of the church had come to see her while she was working for Mrs. Gable that morning. He wanted her to know what was going on in the factory and that it needn't change their lives.

"It seems that this church is trying to find ways to help people who've been out of work so long. One man, a retired factory worker, is real good at making toys out of woods -- things like doll furniture, little trucks, and blocks. So Mr. Gable's letting them use this end of the factory to start a business. They hope it grows and that more people can find work."

"I didn't know churches did stuff like that," Jody said.

"I guess I didn't either," his mother answered. "But you and I've not had much acquaintance with church doings for a long time."

They were eating their butterscotch ice cream when Carlos came to the door, with Tim behind him. "It's coming, Jody," he said. "I ran ahead so you could see."

It took nearly an hour to park the cream-colored house trailer. The movers and Mr. Mendez set it on blocks and worked to get it level.

Mr. Gable came and told Carlos' father that he'd have pipes laid for water the next day. Then he turned to Jody and said, "Tell your mother we'll run some to the caboose while we're at it. I got a small sink that will fit in the counter."

Tim rode back with Mr. Gable and after the movers left the excitement died down. Carlos showed Jody around the three-room trailer. "Is it not fine?" he asked.

"It sure is," Jody answered. "Well, I'd better go. I have homework. See you."

Jody worked at the table in the soft white light of the flower-shaded lamp. His mother patched an elbow in one of his shirts and then she made a pitcher of tea. "With the refrigerator we can have it iced," she said.

"It sure is nice," Jody said. "I could live here forever."

His mother turned and sat down across the table from him. "Jody-boy," she said. "There's something I have to tell you. I got a letter from your father today. The landlady at the apartment house stopped me as I went to work."

Jody felt a choking in his throat. He didn't want bad times to come again. He wished the safe feeling he'd had lately would go on and on. He looked at his mother to see if the sad look was coming back into her eyes. He hoped not. It hadn't been there for a lot of days. Not since they'd moved into the blue caboose really.

"Is he coming back?" Jody asked.

His mother shook her head. "Not now. He has a job in Colorado. And he sent twenty dollars. But the best thing in his letter was this part. I'll read it. 'I guess I messed your life up a lot. And been no help to the boy either. I wouldn't blame you no matter what you do -- like getting a divorce. But for now I'm aiming at one thing. Holding down a job for six months. If I can do that I'll head back to Indiana this fall and see how things stand.'"

"You think that's good?" Jody asked.

"Yes. He's facing his own weakness," his mother said.

"Would you get a divorce, Mom?" Jody asked.

"Not now. Not as long as he's trying to straighten out his life. We're getting along as things are. Have you been worrying about such as that?"

"Well, now and then," Jody said. "A lot of kids talk about stepdads and moms."

"What do they say?" his mother asked.

"Oh!" Jody said. "Stuff like how things

get worse instead of better."

His mother smiled even though tears glistened in her eyes. "I've not hidden much from you, have I, Jody?"

"Well, maybe some. But a lot of times I knew you were worried."

"I was only trying to protect you," she said. "I didn't fool you much, I see."

"Jody looked around at the blue walls and the roses on the lamp and the soft white curtains. "I'd hate to leave this place."

"So would I," his mother said. "And we won't until something better is in front of us. Until it seems right. And that time will come."

Jody knew she was right. They couldn't stay here forever. They'd need more room whether his father came back or not. But that time wasn't now.

"Well, I know one thing," Jody said. "I'll never forget this blue caboose."

His mother smiled. Her eyes were bright in the lamplight. "No, I don't reckon you ever will. And neither will I."

134

The Author

Dorothy Hamilton was born and lives in Delaware County, Indiana. She received her elementary and secondary education in the schools of Cowan and Muncie, Indiana. She also attended Ball State University, Muncie, and has taken work by correspondence from Indiana University, Bloomington, Indiana. She also has attended professional writing courses at various times.

Mrs. Hamilton grew up in the Methodist Church and participated in numerous school, community, and church activities until the youngest of her seven children was married.

Then she was led by prayer-induced direction into service as a private tutor. In a real sense this service was a mission of love. More than 260 girls and boys have come to Mrs. Hamilton for gentle encouragement, for renewal of self-esteem, and to learn to work.

The experience of being a mother and a tutor inspired Mrs. Hamilton in much of her writing.

Seven of her stories have been published by quarterlies, including the Ball State University **Forum.** One story, "The Runaway," was nominated for the American Literary Anthology. She has had published fifty serials, fifty-five short stories, and several articles in religious publications since February 1967. She has written for radio and newspapers. She is author of **Anita's Choice** (1971), **Christmas for Holly** (1971), **Charco** (1971), **The Killdeer** (1971), **Tony Savala** (1972), and **Jim Musco** (1972).

135